MW01259150

A TRUE BOOK™

TECHNOLOGY OF THE AMERICAN CIVIL WAR

Felicia Brower

Children's Press®
An imprint of Scholastic Inc.

Special thanks to our consultant, Dr. Le'Trice Donaldson, Assistant Professor of History, Auburn University, for making sure the text of the book is authentic and historically accurate.

Library of Congress Cataloging-in-Publication Data available

ISBN 978-1-5461-3628-6 (library binding) | ISBN 978-1-5461-3629-3 (paperback) | ISBN 978-1-5461-3630-9 (ebook)

10 9 8 7 6 5 4 3 2 1   25 26 27 28 29

Printed in China 62
First edition, 2025

Design by Kathleen Petelinsek
Series produced by Spooky Cheetah Press

Front cover: Large weapons, like these artillery pieces at Yorktown, Virginia, were used in the Civil War.

Back cover: A Civil War ambulance

Find the Truth!

Everything you are about to read is true *except* for one of the sentences on this page.

Which one is **TRUE**?

T or F Women served as nurses from the start of the Civil War.

T or F Hot-air balloons were used for spying during the war.

Find the answers in this book.

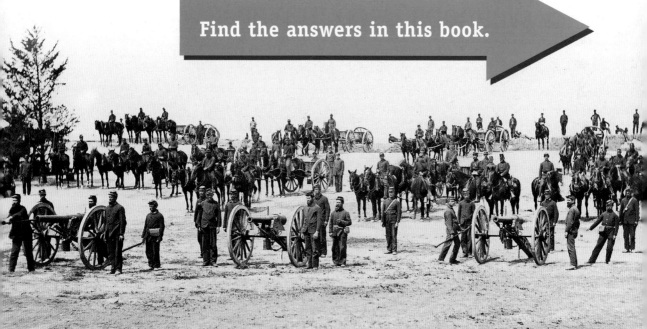

What's in This Book?

This large gun
is a cannon.

The **BIG** Truth

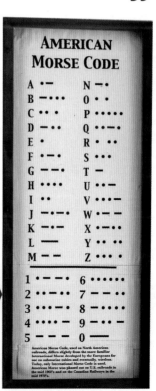

AMERICAN
MORSE CODE

A	·—	N	—·
B	—···	O	··
C	···	P	·····
D	—··	Q	··—·
E	·	R	· ··
F	·—·	S	···
G	——·	T	—
H	····	U	··—
I	··	V	···—
J	—·—·	W	·——
K	—·—	X	·—··
L	——	Y	·· ··
M	——	Z	··· ·

1	·—— ·	6	······
2	··—··	7	——··
3	···—·	8	—····
4	····—	9	—··—
5	———	0	—

American Morse Code, used on North American
railroads, differs slightly from the more familiar
International Morse developed by the Europeans for
use on submarine cables and eventually, wireless.
Today, only International Morse Code is used.
American Morse was phased out on U.S. railroads in
the mid 1960's and on the Canadian Railways in the
mid 1970's.

Morse code was used during the war.

INTRODUCTION

The American Civil War was fought from **1861** to **1865** between the United States of America and the rebellious government calling itself the **Confederate States of America**. The two sides were also known as the **Union** and the **Confederacy—or the Rebels**.

These cannons were set up to defend Washington, D.C., in case of attack.

The conflict tested the strength of the young country. It also marked the start of a new era in warfare. Some **new technologies** from the Civil War, like **more accurate weapons**, made it the deadliest conflict ever. Others, such as **advances in transportation, communication,** and **medical care**, made life better for Americans.

The Civil War started six weeks after President Abraham Lincoln was **inaugurated.**

Troops would sometimes have to march up to 25 miles (40 kilometers) in one day.

This photo shows a reenactment of Union soldiers marching into battle.

Getting Around

The Civil War was fought across the American South all the way to Texas in the West. There were no cars, trucks, or airplanes in 1861. Moving troops and supplies on land was one of the biggest challenges faced by both armies. Soldiers and equipment had to move over many miles, often in terrible conditions. The troops were tired, sore, and sometimes injured when they finally arrived at the battlefield. Advances in transportation made it easier to get soldiers and equipment to battle sites.

All Aboard!

The Civil War was the first war to rely on railroads for military use. Railroads could move soldiers and supplies faster than any other method of transportation. Trains were also more dependable. They worked in any weather.

This illustration shows soldiers taking a train home from the battlefield.

Because railroads were so important, armies often attacked railroad cars and tracks.

Almost every battle east of the Mississippi River was fought within 20 miles (32.1 kilometers) of a railroad. The North had a large railroad network. The Union controlled 20,000 miles (32,186.9 km) of track. The rebelling states had only 9,000 miles (14,484.1 km) of track. This gave the Union an advantage. It could restock supplies and move troops faster than its opponent.

War on the Water

Rivers also provided important transportation routes during the war. This was especially true in the regions around the Mississippi River. Each side sought to control those waterways, as well as coastal **ports**. Steamboats were used to transport men and supplies on rivers. As in previous wars, wooden ships were used to fight battles on water.

Two advances made during the Civil War marked the start of a new era in naval warfare. The first was the use of ironclad warships on rivers and in coastal areas. These vessels had armor made from thick plates of iron or steel. They were much harder to destroy than wooden ships. The second advance was an early version of the submarine, which was used by the Confederate army to launch attacks from under water.

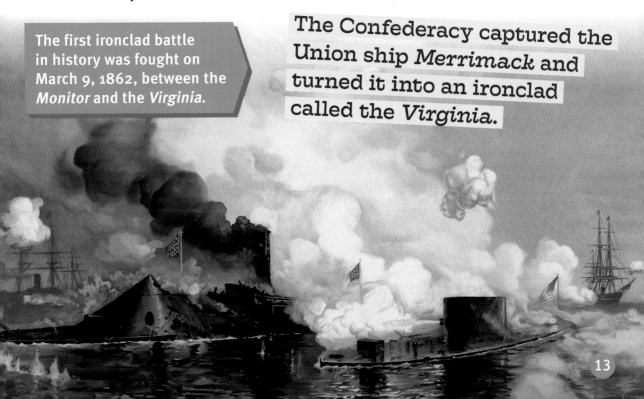

The first ironclad battle in history was fought on March 9, 1862, between the *Monitor* and the *Virginia*.

The Confederacy captured the Union ship *Merrimack* and turned it into an ironclad called the *Virginia*.

Samuel Morse invented the telegraph almost 30 years before the start of the Civil War.

This wagon housed a Union field telegraph office.

Spreading the Word

Communication is crucial during any war. Soldiers receive their orders from commanding officers. Generals have to coordinate attacks and update one another about the situation on the ground. They have to order supplies. Before the Civil War, messages were carried by soldiers either on horseback or on foot. It was a slow and dangerous process. During the war, both sides used existing technology, such as the telegraph, in new ways. They also developed brand-new methods of communication that were more efficient.

Dots and Dashes

The telegraph used electrical signals that traveled over wires to send messages, called telegrams. The messages were transmitted in Morse code, which stood for letters and numbers. Telegrams could be sent quickly over long distances. The Civil War marked the first time this technology was used in a war. The Union army had a larger telegraph network than the Confederacy did. That gave the North another advantage over the enemy.

Running wire for the telegraph

AMERICAN MORSE CODE

A	•—	N	—•
B	—•••	O	• •
C	•• •	P	•••••
D	—••	Q	••—•
E	•	R	• ••
F	•—•	S	•••
G	——•	T	—
H	••••	U	••—
I	••	V	•••—
J	—•—•	W	•——
K	—•—	X	•—••
L	——	Y	•• ••
M	——	Z	••• •

1	•— —•	6	••••••
2	••—••	7	——••
3	•••—•	8	—••••
4	••••—	9	—••—
5	———	0	———

American Morse Code, used on North American railroads, differs slightly from the more familiar International Morse developed by the Europeans for use on submarine cables and eventually, wireless. Today, only International Morse Code is used. American Morse was phased out on U.S. railroads in the mid 1960's and on the Canadian Railways in the mid 1970's.

In Morse code, each letter and number is made up of a combination of dots and dashes.

Cracking the Code

Sending messages by telegraph was risky because they could be stolen by the enemy. That's why both sides used codes and ciphers to keep the content of their messages a secret. For example, Union telegraph operators sent scrambled messages. Only the person on the receiving end had instructions for unscrambling the text. In some cases, a word or symbol was used to represent another word (like *glaze = headquarters*). The Confederate army often used cipher wheels like the one shown here to send messages.

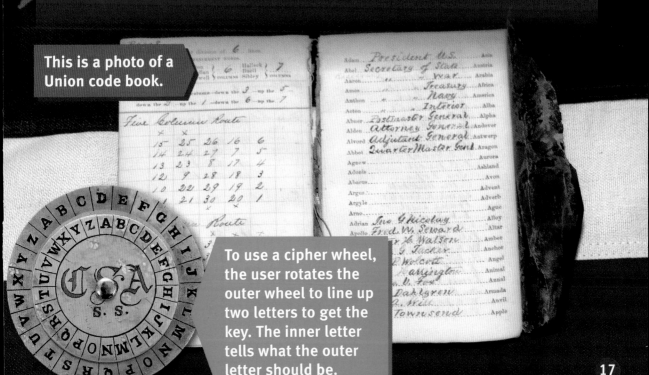

This is a photo of a Union code book.

To use a cipher wheel, the user rotates the outer wheel to line up two letters to get the key. The inner letter tells what the outer letter should be.

17

A Bird's-Eye View

Thaddeus Lowe was a hot-air balloonist who figured out how to transmit a telegram from up in the air. On June 16, 1861, he demonstrated the process for President Lincoln—who quickly realized how useful balloons could be for spying on the enemy. A person in a balloon could see much farther than someone on land and could report on troop strength and position.

This photo shows two hot-air balloons from the Union Army Balloon Corps, which was formed after the first battle of the Civil War.

Thaddeus Lowe is known as the grandfather of the U.S. Air Force.

A Union soldier signals an assault as generals discuss strategy.

Going the Distance

The Signal Corps is a special unit within the army that was created in 1860. During the Civil War, soldiers who belonged to this unit used flags or torches to relay messages across long distances. Different flag or torch movements stood for different letters and numbers. This system was effective because messages could be sent—and received—despite the noise of battle. However, it could be used only on clear days.

Showing the Scenes

Photography was a new invention in the early 1800s. By 1861, the process of taking photos had improved enough that the Civil War would be the first to be photographed extensively. Many photographs from that era are of soldiers preparing to head off to war. These keepsakes were treasured by families left behind.

A Union soldier in camp

This photo shows Columbia, South Carolina, in ruins.

However, photos of the war itself had the biggest impact on Americans. Civil War photographers took thousands of photos of the aftermath of battles. The photos showed destroyed landscapes and fields covered with dead soldiers. For the first time, people could begin to understand the horrors of war. The work of these photographers did a lot to shape public opinion of the conflict.

Mathew Brady is the most famous Civil War photographer.

An estimated 620,000 soldiers died in the Civil War.

Civil War reenactors shooting muskets

Weapons Used in War

Muskets, called long guns, and **artillery**, which are large guns such as cannons, were used by both sides during the war. At the beginning, they had a smooth **barrel** and were loaded from the front (or the muzzle). Both were hard to load and were not very accurate at long distances. As the war progressed, so did the weaponry. Guns became more accurate at greater distances, but the soldiers were still fighting up close. That played a big part in the massive loss of life in the Civil War.

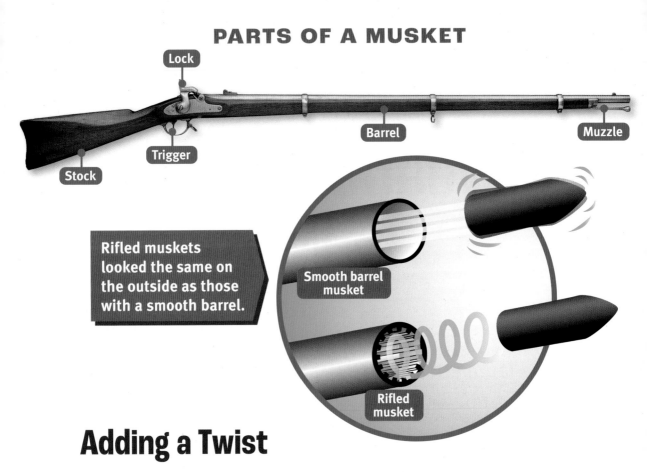

PARTS OF A MUSKET

Lock

Trigger

Stock

Barrel

Muzzle

Rifled muskets looked the same on the outside as those with a smooth barrel.

Smooth barrel musket

Rifled musket

Adding a Twist

Before long, both armies had moved from muskets with a smooth barrel to rifled muskets, which had spiral grooves inside the barrel. That enabled the gun to fire more accurately at a greater distance. The Civil War was the first time in history when most **infantrymen** carried rifled guns.

A Deadly Bullet

Bullets for muskets were round, solid pieces of metal that caused small wounds. During the Civil War, a new type of bullet gained popularity—the minié ball. Among other features, that bullet had a pointed tip and a hollow base. The minié ball expanded as it exited the gun, causing larger wounds and often shattering bones. The new bullet contributed to the estimated 60,000 **amputations** performed during the war.

The minié ball was invented by a French army officer named Claude-Étienne Minié in 1849.

Musket ball

Minié ball

Three-quarters of all operations during the war were amputations.

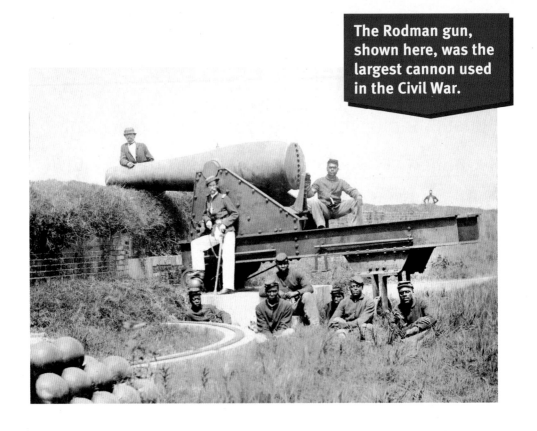

Artillery: The Big Guns

Cannons played an important role in the Civil War. As with muskets, the change from smooth barrel to rifled made cannons more effective. These extremely large and heavy field guns fired heavy **projectiles** at the enemy. A simple cannonball was a solid round shot that was usually fired at enemy artillery or fortifications.

Case shot was another type of projectile. It was used against soldiers. Case shot was a hollow shell that was filled with pieces of metal called shrapnel. After the case shot left the cannon, it burst in the air, spraying shrapnel over a large area. Grapeshot, or small metal balls, was used when soldiers fought at close range. The Gatling gun was another innovative artillery piece. It had multiple barrels.

The early Gatling gun fired up to 200 bullets per minute.

Soldiers fired the Gatling gun by turning a crank handle.

More accurate guns gave rise to a new type of soldier: a sharpshooter.

Breech

Sharpshooters could hit an enemy from a hidden position very far away. Today those soldiers are called snipers.

Reload!

Later in the war, long guns were improved again by the introduction of breech-loading rifles. These rifles could be reloaded from the breech, or back, of the barrel instead of through the front of the barrel. To save time and money, factories started making **standardized** parts for weapons. If one part of a rifle broke, it could be swapped out.

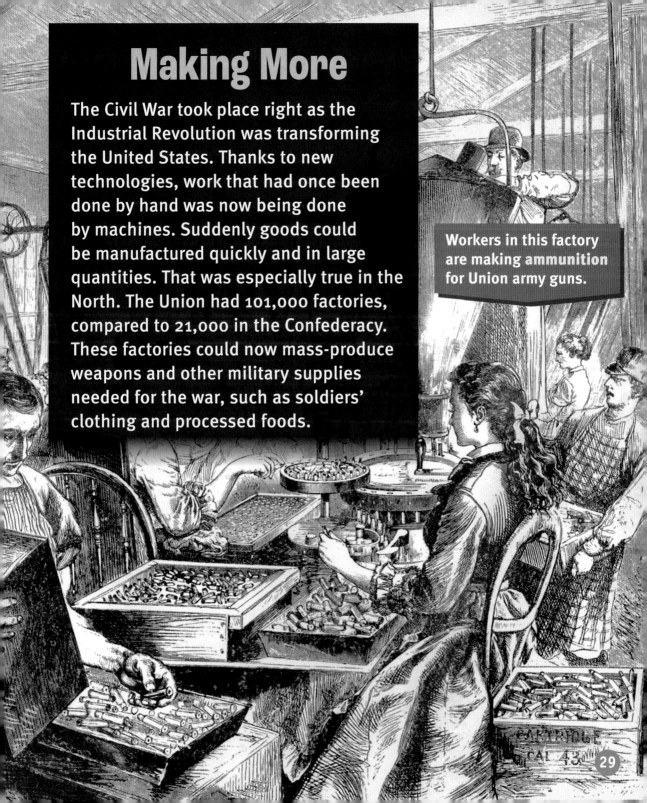

Making More

The Civil War took place right as the Industrial Revolution was transforming the United States. Thanks to new technologies, work that had once been done by hand was now being done by machines. Suddenly goods could be manufactured quickly and in large quantities. That was especially true in the North. The Union had 101,000 factories, compared to 21,000 in the Confederacy. These factories could now mass-produce weapons and other military supplies needed for the war, such as soldiers' clothing and processed foods.

Workers in this factory are making **ammunition** for Union army guns.

New Orleans was the first major Confederate city to be taken by Union forces.

Floating mine

Explosive Devices

At the time of the Civil War, bombs and other explosive devices were all known as "torpedoes." Those included grenades, which were thrown at the enemy, as well as land mines and floating mines. Some mines exploded into fragments when touched; others were activated remotely.

An explosive called a coal torpedo was made to **sabotage** trains and ships, both of which were powered by burning coal. Coal torpedoes looked like coal, but were hollow iron shells filled with explosives. Soldiers would hide coal torpedoes among the enemy's coal supply. When the torpedoes were shoveled into a train's or ship's firebox, they would explode.

This Union train was a victim of Confederate sabotage.

Piece of coal

Coal torpedo

Unsung Heroes: Horses in War

The cavalry is a unit of soldiers on horseback.
Advances in technology during the Civil War made
fighting on horseback impractical, but horses and
mules remained the lifeblood of both sides.
Here's how they were used.

Three million horses and mules
served during the Civil War.

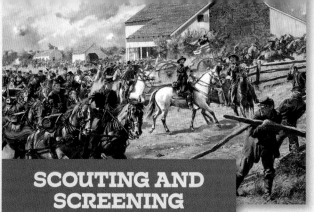

SCOUTING AND SCREENING

The cavalry was mainly used for scouting. Soldiers on horseback would ride ahead of the army to find out the enemy's position and strength. The cavalry also rode alongside the infantrymen to screen them from the enemy.

TRANSPORTATION

Horses and mules were used to pull loads that were too heavy for soldiers to move. They pulled cannons and the wagons that held the heavy ammunition for the cannons. Horses and mules were also used to pull wagons that transported food, medical supplies, and other essentials.

COMMUNICATION

Messages that needed to be sent quickly were often delivered by soldiers on horseback when faster methods weren't available.

About two-thirds of all soldiers who died during the war died from diseases such as dysentery—or bloody diarrhea—not from their wounds.

A field hospital in Gettysburg, Pennsylvania

Staying Alive

Advances in weapons, ammunition, and tactics led to a staggering number of **casualties**. Many soldiers suffered from battle wounds. Even more died from infectious diseases, which are diseases that spread rapidly. The medicines that fight or prevent the spread of infectious diseases hadn't been invented yet. It became clear early on that more medical staff was needed—as well as improved treatments. Medical advances made during this time paved the way for progress in overall health care for the public after the war.

This wagon was specially made to transport wounded soldiers.

How to Save a Life

Treating wounded soldiers on the battlefield was nearly impossible. The need to transport them to hospitals led to the creation of the United States Ambulance Corps, which was staffed by people with first-aid experience. A new lightweight ambulance wagon was developed that made transporting the wounded safer and easier.

So many soldiers were wounded in battle that a system had to be set up to figure out who to treat first. Triage was the method medics used to sort wounded soldiers. Those who were badly injured but had a good chance of survival got first priority. They were taken by ambulance wagons to field hospitals and hospital trains before others.

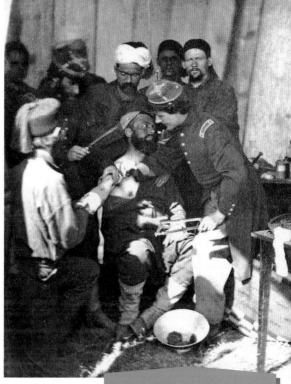

A Union doctor tends to a wounded soldier.

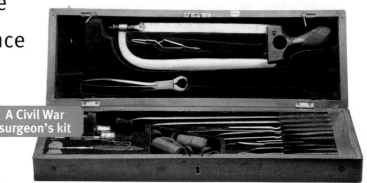

A Civil War surgeon's kit

The Civil War triage categories were slight, mild, severe, and mortal wounds. Severe wounds were given priority.

Nurses to the Rescue

At the beginning of the war, only men were allowed to be nurses.

As casualties mounted and more help was needed to offer care to the wounded, women were allowed to join the war effort as nurses. In addition to providing basic medical care, such as changing bandages, nurses lifted soldiers' spirits. They read to soldiers and helped them write letters home. Some women were in charge of cleaning dirty bedding, which improved **sanitation** and reduced infection.

Timeline: Technological Milestones of the Civil War

APRIL 1861
The U.S. Military Telegraph Corps is established.

OCTOBER 1861
The Union Army Balloon Corps is established.

MARCH 8–9, 1862
Ironclad ships are used in warfare for the first time.

AUGUST 2, 1862
The United States Ambulance Corps is created.

Paving the Way to the Future

Advances made before and during the Civil War had a huge impact on how the war was fought and the number of casualties that resulted. Those technologies paved the way for modern warfare. Some technological advances also improved the lives of everyday Americans—from better methods of transportation and communication to improved medical care. People today continue to benefit from—and build upon—these technological innovations.

SEPTEMBER 1862
The first-ever photographs of war casualties are taken.

FEBRUARY 17, 1864
The Confederate *H.L. Hunley* becomes the first combat submarine to sink a ship.

SPRING 1864
Gatling guns are used for the first time in battle by the Union army.

Mathew Brady
(1822–1896)

Brady was the first photographer to document a war. Under his direction, a team of photographers captured thousands of images of the Civil War. Their photos forever changed how people understood the tragedy of war.

Clara Barton
(1821–1912)

Barton, a former teacher, traveled with the Union army, helping injured Union soldiers as well as captured Confederate soldiers. She also fought for improved medical care for soldiers with better sanitation, supplies, and treatment within the military hospitals.

Dorothea Dix
(1802–1887)

Dix, who was the superintendent of army nurses for the Union army, was known for her strict standards and training for potential nurses. She believed that every wounded soldier who needed help deserved proper care, so her nurses often treated both Union and captured Confederate soldiers.

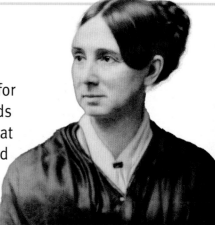

James Henry Gooding (1838–1864)

AND

George E. Stephens (c. 1832–1888)

Gooding and Stephens served in the 54th Massachusetts (shown here), one of the first Black regiments to be formed during the Civil War. They also acted as war correspondents and published eyewitness reports from the battlefields.

Allan Pinkerton (1818–1894)

In 1850, Pinkerton founded the Pinkerton National Detective Agency, which specialized in preventing train robberies. Pinkerton was in charge of protecting Abraham Lincoln as the president-elect traveled to Washington, D.C., in 1861, and he served as the intelligence officer for the Union army during the Civil War.

Antoine Scott (unknown–1878)

Scott, a member of the Ottawa and Ojibwa nations, was part of Company K (shown here). Company K was the only company of Indigenous men in a Union sharpshooter regiment. Scott was recommended twice for the Medal of Honor for good conduct, gallantry, and bravery during the war.

Eyewitness to History

Historians use primary sources to study the past. These are documents such as letters, manuscripts, diaries, photographs, and newspaper stories created during the time under study. Here are two primary sources from the Civil War that offer a glimpse of what life was like during that time.

NOT ALL CIVIL WAR INNOVATIONS were technological advances. Sometimes they were just good ideas. During the course of the war, both armies used "Quaker guns" to fool the enemy. Quakers are people who belong to a religious group that is opposed to war. Quaker guns were really logs that had been painted and mounted to look like cannons from far away. Quaker guns were used many times during the war to keep enemy troops from attacking or to give soldiers time to escape an advancing army.

This photograph shows the use of "Quaker guns" on a battlefield. Do they look like guns to you? →

THE USE OF THE TELEGRAPH during the Civil War made it possible for President Lincoln to communicate directly with his generals practically in real time. In fact, the president slept on a cot in the telegraph office during important battles. Lincoln also used the telegraph to discover what officers were saying to one another. In 1864, Lincoln saw correspondence between Union General Ulysses S. Grant and his superior officer General Henry Halleck during the siege of Petersburg, Virginia. Halleck wanted Grant to move some of his soldiers to Washington, D.C., to guard the city. Grant refused. Lincoln sent this telegram to Grant.

The telegram from President Lincoln to Grant reads: "I have seen your dispatch expressing your unwillingness to break your hold where you are. Neither am I willing. Hold on with a bull-dog grip, and chew and choke, as much as possible."

Executive Mansion,

Washington, August 17, 1864.

Lieut. Gen. Grant
City Point, Va.

I have seen your dispatch expressing your unwillingness to break your hold where you are. Neither am I willing. Hold on with a bull-dog grip, and chew & choke, as much as possible.

A. Lincoln

True Statistics

How long the Civil War lasted: 4 years, 1 month, and 2 weeks

Number of soldiers who fought: More than 2.8 million

Number of soldiers who died: About 620,000

Deadliest day: Battle of Antietam (about 22,700 casualties total)

Number of factories in the Union: 101,000

Number of factories in the Confederacy: 21,000

Miles of telegraph lines installed during the war: 15,000

Number of rifles made in the North during the war: 1.5 million

Number of hospitals at the end of the Civil War: About 400

Did you find the truth?

F Women served as nurses from the start of the Civil War.

T Hot-air balloons were used for spying during the war.

Resources

Other books in this series:

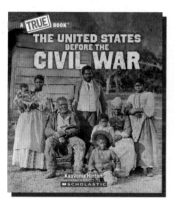 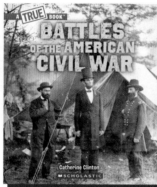 

You can also look at:

Bearce, Stephanie. *Top Secret Files: The Civil War: Spies, Secret Missions, and Hidden Facts from the Civil War*. Abingdon, U.K.: Routledge, 2021.

Benoit, Peter. *The Civil War*. New York: Scholastic, 2011.

Mara, Wil. *If You Were a Kid During the Civil War*. New York: Scholastic, 2016.

Mattern, Joanne. *Technology During the Civil War*. Minnesota: ABDO Publishing, 2016.

Patrick, Denise Lewis. *If You Lived During the Civil War*. New York: Scholastic, 2022.

Glossary

ammunition (am-yuh-NISH-uhn) things such as bullets or shells that can be fired from weapons

amputations (am-pyoo-TAY-shuhnz) the removal of people's limbs

artillery (ahr-TIL-ur-ee) large, powerful guns that are mounted on wheels or tracks

barrel (BAR-uhl) the tube-shaped part at the front of a gun

casualties (KAZH-oo-uhl-teez) people who are injured or killed in a war

inaugurated (in-AW-gyuh-ray-ted) sworn into office

infantrymen (IN-fuhn-tree-men) the foot soldiers of an army

ports (ports) harbors or places where boats and ships can dock or anchor safely

projectiles (pruh-JEK-tuhlz) objects, such as bullets or missiles, that are thrown or shot through the air

sabotage (SAB-uh-tahzh) the deliberate damage or destruction of property, especially to prevent or stop something

sanitation (san-i-TAY-shuhn) the prevention of disease by maintenance of clean conditions

standardized (STAN-dur-dizd) produced in a consistent way

Index

Page numbers in **bold** indicate illustrations.

About the Author

Felicia Brower is a writer living in Denver, Colorado. She loves uncovering interesting stories from history and seeing how what we've learned from the past can help us create a brighter future.